SLEEPING BEAUTY

Along time ago and and in a land far away there lived a King and a Queen. They were very happy, for their first child, a much longed for little girl, had been born. The King ordered that a grand christening should be held for her, for he was delighted to have a daughter.

Everyone who was anyone was invited to the christening – their relatives and friends, all the noble men and women of the land, and royalty from neighbouring kingdoms too. People talked about it throughout the kingdom, for it was to be a great

celebration.

"We must invite all the fairies of the kingdom to bless her," said the Queen.

"How many are there now?" asked the King.

"Twelve or thirteen," said his wife. "Send out the invitations. We'll soon find out."

There were twelve fairies, and they were all sent invitations. A thirteenth fairy had not been heard of for so long that it was presumed that she was dead. No invitation was sent.

The day of the christening was sunny and bright. The tiny Princess was named Briar Rose, and the fairies began to give their gifts.

"She shall be beautiful," said the first.

"She shall be wise," said the second.

"She shall be good," said the third.

"She shall be kind," said the fourth.

The gifts continued in this way, wishing all that was good for Briar Rose. Eleven of the twelve fairies had given their gifts and the twelfth was about to take her place by the royal cradle when the room suddenly went dark. There was a great flash of light which blinded the whole assembly, and when everyone could see again a small dark figure stood in front of the King and Queen.

It was the thirteenth fairy and she did not look at all pleased.

"Why wasn't I invited to the christening?" she screamed at the King and Queen.

Naturally she was furious at being left out and gave them no chance to explain.

"All the fairies of the kingdom have given their blessings. Well, here's mine for the Princess! On her

sixteenth birthday she will prick her finger on a spinning wheel and die!"

With another flash of light the fairy was gone.

"But we thought she was dead!" said the King aghast.

"Oh, what can we do?" The Queen was in tears.

The twelfth fairy stepped forward.

"There is still my gift for Briar Rose," she said. "The fairy's curse cannot be undone,

but I can soften it a little. She will prick her finger, but instead of dying she will fall into a deep sleep that will last one hundred years."

There was a great hubbub in the hall as everyone

discussed the events. The following day the King issued a proclamation, ordering that all spinning wheels and spindles were to be destroyed. Throughout the land there were great fires as the spinning wheels were burned.

Over the years, the Princess grew into a lovely girl. All who met her were enchanted by her.

Eventually, the bad fairy's wish was forgotten. All spinning wheels and spindles had

been destroyed, so there was no reminder. And the thirteenth fairy was not heard of again.

And so, on Briar Rose's sixteenth birthday, the King and Queen were due to arrive back from a far away visit. There was to be a large birthday party for the Princess.

Briar Rose was wandering around the palace. Everyone was preparing for the party, so she could please herself where she went. As there were still parts of the palace that she had never set foot in, she decided to go exploring.

"I wonder what is in the Great South Tower," she said to herself. All the servants and courtiers wished her a happy birthday as she made her way across the palace.

That part of the palace was very old, and there were very few people there. The

base of the tower was in a corridor. The entrance was a small, very solid looking door. The key was on the outside.

"It's very stiff," said the Princess, as she turned the key. "There! It's open!"

Stairs led up the tower in front of her. She began to climb them.

Meanwhile, the King and Queen and the royal party had arrived back at the palace in time for the day's celebrations.

"Has anyone seen the Princess?" asked the King. "Today is her sixteenth birthday – the day when the curse may fall. Somebody must know where she is!"

Nearly everyone had seen her, but nobody knew where she had been going.

"She must be found," said the frantic Queen, wringing her hands anxiously. "If the fairy's evil prophecy is to come true, then today is the day! Oh, where can she be?"

A search of the palace and the grounds began without further delay.

Meanwhile, the Princess had reached the top of the old, deserted tower where there was yet another

door. This time there was no key but the
wooden door was slightly open.

"There must be a wonderful view of the
rest of the palace and grounds from the
window," thought the young Princess.

Then she heard a strange whirring sound.
It was unlike anything that she had ever heard

before.

She pushed the door open and went into
the room. There, in the middle, sat an old
woman working at a spinning wheel. Behind
her was an enormous bed.

The wheel was making the noise.

"What are you doing?" asked Briar Rose. "I
have never seen one of those before, what is it?"

"It is a spinning wheel," said the old woman.
"Would you like to try it my dear?"

"Oh, may I?" asked Briar Rose.

She sat on the stool in front of the wheel and the wheel whirred round. As soon as she touched the spindle she pricked her finger. She fell to the floor in a deep sleep. The old woman, who was really the wicked thirteenth fairy in disguise, picked her up and laid her on the bed.

At that moment, all over the palace, people began to fall asleep. The cooks who were preparing for the party fell asleep over the stirring and tasting. The scullery maids fell asleep over the washing up. The laundry maid fell asleep over her washing. The chamber maids fell asleep while they dusted, polished and prepared for the party.

The King and Queen, the courtiers and the guests fell asleep in the Great Hall. The

guards fell asleep at their posts. The search parties looking for the Princess fell asleep while they searched – in the gardens, in the corridors, in the spare rooms, and some in the oldest part of the palace.

Even the flies fell asleep on the stable walls. The birds and the butterflies fell asleep in the palace gardens. So did the wild rabbits that raided the palace vegetable gardens. The gardeners and their helpers, who were busy chasing off the rabbits, fell asleep in mid-chase.

In the hearths the fires died down and the meat stopped cooking. The kitchen maid stopped plucking the chicken.

The entire palace fell asleep, along with the Princess.

A hedge of briar roses sprang up around the palace, protecting it from the outside world.

Years passed, and from time to time a King's son would come to

the famous briar hedge to try and find the mysterious sleeping Princess that legend spoke of. But none got through. The hedge was too strong and the Princes were cut to bits.

A hundred years passed and the tale of the Sleeping Beauty, as the Princess was known, became a great legend. Very few people believed she really existed.

One day a King's son came to the nearby village.

"Legend says –" an old man was speaking in the village square

– "legend says that the Princess lies asleep behind that great briar hedge just outside the village. In my grandfather's day, you could see the topmost turret of her tower, so they say."

The Prince stopped to listen. "Where can I find this hedge?" he asked.

"Just beyond the village, young sir," said the old man. "If you're going to try, you'll need more luck than the other young men who have gone before you."

"I shall try," said the Prince. "We have heard of Sleeping Beauty in my kingdom too. She is said to be beautiful and kind beyond words."

The Prince went to the hedge and held up his sword. He went to strike at the hedge, but where his sword met the thorns, great roses bloomed instead. A path

opened for him, for the one hundred years were up. The curse was lifting and the hedge seemed to disappear before him.

He went through into the palace grounds, walking past the sleeping rabbits, birds and butterflies, and the gardeners at their work. The kitchens were full of cooks and maids who hadn't moved for a hundred years – they were all fast asleep. Even the King and Queen who were seated at the table in the Great Hall were sleeping soundly!

The Prince walked on through the palace, making his way to the tallest tower where he climbed the stairs and entered the tower room.

There on the bed he saw Briar Rose fast asleep.

"She is so lovely," he said softly to himself. He had fallen completely in love with her. "How can I wake her?"

He leant over and gently kissed her.

Briar Rose's eyelids flickered and she woke up. The first person she saw was the handsome Prince and she fell in love with him on the spot.

Together they walked down to the Great Hall, hand in hand. The King and Queen were just waking up when the Prince and Briar Rose entered.

The cooks in the kitchen woke up to carry on preparing the food and the chambermaids and other servants carried on with their work too as if nothing had ever happened.

The party was still to be held, but it now it was to be an engagement party instead of a birthday party. The Prince and Briar Rose were to be married.

The hedge disappeared and the villagers saw the palace again and realised the legend had been true after all.

And as for the bad fairy? Well, she was never heard of again!

THE FROG PRINCE

Once upon a time there lived a King who had several beautiful daughters, but the youngest was even more beautiful than the rest. Near the castle of this King was a large and gloomy forest. Just a short walk into the trees was a small clearing. And at the far side stood an old lime tree, and beneath its branches splashed a fountain in the middle of a dark, deep pool.

Whenever it was very hot, the King's youngest daughter would run off into this wood and sit by the pool, throwing her golden ball into the air. This was her favourite pastime.

19

One afternoon when the Princess threw the ball high up in the air, she didn't catch it! It slipped through her fingers onto the grass. Then it rolled past her into the pool and disappeared beneath the water.

The Princess peered into the pool, but her precious ball was gone. Quickly, she plunged her arms into the pool as far as she could reach, but she could feel nothing except weeds and water lilies. Some people said the pool was so deep it had no

bottom. So when the Princess realised her golden ball was gone forever, she began to cry. "Come back to me this minute, golden ball," sobbed the Princess, staring into the water.

Now as a rule, Princesses are used to getting their own way. So after her golden ball didn't magically pop up out of the water, she started to howl even louder. Dear, oh dear! First she stamped her feet and then she threw herself down on the grass in temper.

The Princess was making so much noise that she didn't notice a big,

20

green frog stick his head out of the water and jump onto the grass beside her.

"Don't cry, beautiful Princess," croaked the frog. "I saw your golden ball fall into the water, and it will be my pleasure to dive down and get it for you, if you will give me something in return."

At this, the Princess cheered up. "I will gladly give you all my jewels and pearls, even my golden crown, if you will bring back my golden ball."

(It is true to say that promises should never be made in a hurry, even by Princesses, because a promise is a thing that must be kept, especially to frogs!)

The frog hopped nearer to the Princess. "Pearls and jewels and golden crowns are no use to me," he went on, "but if you will love me and be my friend, if you will let me eat from your golden plate, drink from your golden cup, and sleep on your golden bed, I will gladly dive down and fetch your ball."

So eager was the Princess to see her golden ball once more, that she didn't listen too carefully to what the frog had to say.

"I promise you all you ask, if only you will bring my ball," she said.

Quick as a flash, the frog jumped into the pool then bobbed up again with the ball in his mouth. Straight away the King's daughter snatched her ball and ran back to the castle.

"Take me with you!" cried the frog. "I cannot run as fast as you and I shall be left behind!" But the Princess didn't care about her promise and soon forgot all about the frog. Later that day, when the Princess was sitting at the table, something was heard coming up the marble stairs. Splish, splosh, splish, splosh! The sound came nearer and nearer, and a voice cried, "Let me in, youngest daughter of the King."

The Princess jumped up from the table to see who had called her. Now when she caught sight of the little frog, she turned very pale.

"What does a frog want with you?" demanded the King, looking rather surprised.

The Princess hung her head. "When I was sitting by the fountain my favourite golden ball fell into the water. This frog fetched it back for me, because I cried so much." The Princess started to cry

again. "I promised to love him and let him eat from my golden plate, drink from my golden cup, and sleep on my golden bed."

The King looked at the frog and thought for a while before he spoke. "Then you must keep your promise, my daughter."

The Princess knew she must obey, so she beckoned the frog to come inside. The frog hopped in after her and jumped up into her chair and straight onto the table.

24

"Now push your golden plate near me," said the frog, "so that we may eat together." As she did so, the frog leapt onto her plate and gobbled up all her dinner messily, which was just as well, because the Princess didn't feel much like eating.

Next, the frog drank from her little golden cup, with great slurping noises until it was quite empty. Somehow the Princess didn't feel at all thirsty now either! After the frog had finished, he took one great leap and landed on the Princess's knee.

"Go away you ugly, cold frog!" she cried. "I will never let you sleep on my lovely, clean bed!"

This made the King very angry. "This little frog helped you when you needed it. You made a promise to him and now you must keep it."

"I am very tired after that wonderful meal," the frog said, "and you did promise that I could go to sleep on your golden bed."

Very unwillingly the Princess picked up the frog and carried him up the castle

stairs to her bedroom.

When the ugly frog hopped into the middle of her beautiful golden bed, it was just too much for the young Princess. She tugged hard at the coverlet and tipped the poor frog onto the floor.

As he fell he was changed into a handsome Prince. A spell had been cast on him by an evil witch and only a Princess had the power to break it!

The Princess was
perfectly

speechless. She felt very sorry indeed that she had been so unkind to the frog now that she saw he was a dashing young man.

With the blessing of the King, the handsome (and rather patient!) Prince and the lovely (but rather silly!) Princess were married, and I'm sure lived happily ever after.

THE WILD SWANS

Long ago and far away there lived a King. He was very proud of his eleven sons and one daughter. All of his children were good, kind and wise, even young Eliza who was still only a baby.

The Queen had sadly died and after a while, feeling that his children needed a mother, the King married again.

His new Queen was a mean and selfish lady. She was very jealous of the eleven princes and Eliza, and life for them soon changed. Eliza was sent to the country to be brought up on a farm.

The Queen turned the King from his sons, by telling lies to him about them. Soon the King cared nothing for his sons. The Queen was delighted.

"Go, you big ugly birds," she cried to them one day, casting a spell on them.

But the worst she could do was to turn them into swans with golden crowns on their heads. Away they flew.

They flew over the cottage where Eliza lived, but no-one saw them.

Eliza lived happily at the farm, but she missed her brothers. When she was fifteen, she returned to the palace. Her father, the King, was out hunting, and she was greeted by her nasty stepmother.

The Queen was furious at how pretty Eliza had become. She was jealous of her sweet nature and could not bear that the King should love her more than herself. She would dearly have liked to turn her into a swan like her brothers so that she too

would fly from the palace, but she could not use the same magic spell again.

Instead she bathed Eliza and put three toads in the tub with her to make her ugly. Eliza wondered why she was sharing a bath with the toads, but she was too kind and naïve to question her stepmother. Anyway, to

the Queen's disgust, the ugly toads were instantly turned to poppies by Eliza's innocence and goodness.

Still determined to be rid of her beautiful stepdaughter, the Queen then used walnut juice to darken Eliza's skin, telling her that it was a wonderful new soap, and matted her hair with fat, letting her believe that it would make her hair glossy and thick.

Now, to the Queen's delight,

Eliza looked truly awful indeed.

"This will make the King reject you," said the Queen, and the King did turn from Eliza. He did not know that this messy girl brought before him was his daughter.

Eliza did not now how she looked as she had no mirror to check her appearance and so she was very upset that her father had sent her away. In despair she decided to set off to search for her beloved brothers. She went over the fields and through the forests. She came at last to a stream and saw her own reflection.

"No wonder my father did not know me," she said, and she immediately jumped in to wash herself. Moments later Eliza emerged, once again looking as she should, with clean golden hair and fair skin.

For many days she walked on alone through the countryside, tired and hungry, looking for her brothers. At last, one day she met an old woman. She had a basket of fruit and was kind enough to share some with the hungry young girl.

"Have you seen eleven princes riding through the forest?" asked Eliza.

"I haven't, my dear," said the old woman. "But yesterday I did see eleven swans riding down the stream. Each had a golden crown on his head." She showed Eliza the

river.

Eliza followed the river to the shore, and stood watching the waves. As the sun was setting, eleven swans flew down to the shore. As the sun set, the swans turned into eleven princes with golden crowns on their heads.

"My brothers!" cried Eliza, and she ran to greet them. They were delighted to see their young sister, now grown into a lovely girl. They soon realised that it was because of the wicked Queen that they were rejected.

"We are swans during the day," said the eldest prince. "But when the sun goes down, we regain our human form. We therefore have to be over land when the sun sets or we will be doomed to a watery grave."

"We will take you with us when we leave tomorrow, sweet sister," said the youngest. "But as we will have no hands, tonight we must weave a strong net large enought to carry you."

All night the brothers and sister wove a net. In the morning as Eliza slept, eleven

swans flew up into the air, carrying the net. The youngest shaded Eliza's face from the sun with his wing.

On the other side of the sea was a beautiful land. The brothers flew hard to reach it in daylight.

"Here is your new home," they said as they landed beside a small cave in a forest.

Eliza had a dream that night. A fairy came to her and said, "There is a way to save

your brothers, but it means hardship and pain for you. There are stinging nettles around the cave. Gather them, although they will sting, and trample them with your feet. With the flax, weave and make up eleven mail shirts for your brothers. But you must never speak, from the moment you start until you finish, even if it takes years, or your brothers will die."

38

Eliza awoke with a nettle stinging her hand.

Her brothers had already left as it was broad daylight, so Eliza began her work. When they returned and saw her poor blistered hands, and she would not say a word, they realised that she was working for them. Two more days and the first shirt was finished. A day later, she was at her work, when the royal huntsmen came to the forest. She ran to her cave in fright, but the dogs followed her. The King was amongst the huntsmen and fell in love with beautiful Eliza when he saw her.

"This damp cave is no place for a lovely girl to be living in. If you will let me, I will

take you to the palace, where you may make your home," he told Eliza.

There, Eliza was washed and dressed in beautiful clothes, and the King chose to

make her his Queen, but she would not smile or say a word.

"My present to you," he said, taking her to a small chamber, "is a room like your cave, with all your familiar things around you."

There, Eliza saw the prepared nettles and the completed shirt and she was happy.

Night after night the young Queen crept away from the King to continue her work.

Soon seven shirts were completed, but she had no more flax. Eliza knew that the nearest nettles grew in the graveyard.

At the dead of night, while all were asleep, she crept out to the graveyard. On a gravestone sat seven witches, counting the dead. Eliza walked straight past, with a shudder.

The Archbishop was the only one to have seen Eliza leave, and he had followed

her. He did not trust her, and thought she had bewitched the King.

"The Queen is a witch," the Archbishop told the King. "I have proof."

The King did not want to believe it, but he kept watch to see if Eliza went out at night. Night after night, she continued her weaving in the small room. Then one night, with one shirt to go, Eliza ran out of flax and nettles. She would have to visit the graveyard again. This time the King followed. He saw the witches on the gravestone and believed Eliza to be one of them.

"The people must judge her,"

41

said the King sadly.

And the people judged that she was a witch and should be burned at the stake.

Eliza was thrown into prison. Her pillows and sheets were the nettle shirts. She could not have wished for better blankets, and she continued her work.

Eleven princes arrived that night at the palace gate, demanding to see the King.

"It's too late to disturb the King," said the guards. Eleven swans flew off as dawn broke.

Eliza was carried to the stake in a cart,

still sewing and weaving the eleventh shirt. The others lay at her feet.

"Look at the witch!" cried the mob. "She still sews! She's casting spells. Take the garments from her!"

The people were about to tear the shirts from her when eleven swans appeared, golden crowns on their heads, flapping their wings and forcing the people back.

The executioner went to tie Eliza to the stake, but Eliza quickly threw the shirts over her brothers, and they became princes again. Sadly the youngest still had a wing

instead of an arm, as Eliza had not quite finished the shirt.

"Now I may speak!" cried Eliza, turning to the King.

The whole story was told to the King, who was very happy. He did not want to lose his beautiful and gentle Eliza.

As the eldest prince spoke, the wood at the stake blossomed and a huge rose bush sprang up in its place.

The King gave a rose to Eliza, and there was a happy wedding procession back to the palace, where the King and Eliza lived happily.